HULDA

HULDA

Text by Carol Svendsen

Pictures by Julius Svendsen

HOUGHTON MIFFLIN COMPANY BOSTON/1974

Library of Congress Cataloging in Publication Data

Svendsen, Carol.
  Hulda.

    SUMMARY: Hulda's temper tantrums always get her
what she wants--until the day she meets a troll family.
    [1. Behavior--Fiction. 2. Trolls--Fiction.
3. Stories in rhyme] I. Svendsen, Julius, 1919-
illus. II. Title.
PZ8.3.S992Hu   [E]   74-9375
ISBN 0-395-19497-0

The bold, hardy Vikings were filled with alarm
As they stared at the ground on the Tollefsen farm.
Footprints before never caused much surprise,
But footprints before never were quite this size.
They shuddered, and fled to their homes in dismay
And hoped that the giant would stay far away.

1

And now, meet Miss Hulda, who lived on that farm.
Each one who met her was struck by her charm.
She was ever so pleasant — delightful and charming.
Her manners were lovely — her smile quite disarming.
A sweet little angel, you'd probably say,
And she was, just as long as she got her own way.

But say "No" to Miss Hulda, "You can't," or "Not now,"
Or expect that a matter was settled somehow,
And Hulda would, first of all, raise such a clangor —
A tantrum so filled with wild fury and anger —
That only the bravest found out what came next
And what she would do when she *really* was vexed!

She would then begin screaming — and that was a scream
So terribly, horribly, loud and extreme,
That even the people from five miles away
All knew that Miss Hulda would soon get her way.
So Hulda was pampered and spoiled every day.
The bold, hardy Vikings felt safer that way.

On this day, the day of the footprint display,
Miss Hulda was told she could not have her way.
So, Hulda, of course, began yelling and kicking
For Hulda had planned to go blueberry picking.
"No," said her father, "you can't, no not now."
"The Troll in the forest will find you somehow."
So she started to scream and the house began shaking.
Then ears began aching and things began breaking.

With a flounce of her curls and a bucket to fill
She left for the forest out over the hill.
She passed the Troll footprints with never a glance,
And pity the one who would stop her advance.
They couldn't stop Hulda, no not for a minute.
She marched to the woods, and then she was in it.

Over rock-laden paths; under towering trees

With branches that reached out to seize and to squeeze,

Hulda trudged on, with a frown on her face

And finally arrived at her blueberry place.

Soon her frown was erased by a smile all serene,
As she gazed at the blueberries, fit for a queen.
She soon filled her bucket that fine afternoon
By choosing the plumpest while humming a tune.
Contented and happy, she wasn't prepared
To be suddenly, terribly, thoroughly scared.

For Hulda now faced the most horrible glare
Of a charging, ferocious, atrocious big bear.
Well, Hulda jumped four or five feet in the air,
Her blueberries scattering about everywhere.

But a change in direction spoiled the bear's plans.
He was seized by a pair of enormous-sized hands.
A huge mountain Troll with long shaggy hair
Lifted and held that fierce, snarling bear.

When Hulda dared once again peek at the world
From the blueberry patch where she lay tightly curled,
She looked up at two disapproving Troll eyes,
And oh, how she wished they were not quite that size!
But the thought of her blueberries, juicy and sweet,
Made her so reckless she jumped to her feet.
She reached for her bucket and swung it around,
Hitting the Troll in the midst of his frown.
The Troll was astonished. That just wasn't fair!
So he ran away crying, along with his bear.

What Hulda had done wasn't brave . . . it was mean,
For under the Troll's shaggy hair she had seen
That the giant, though bigger, was younger than she.
He was possibly, barely, well maybe just three.
So Hulda, again, without further delay,
Began blueberry picking, and having her way.
But the look on her face remained stubborn and grim
Till she filled up her bucket once more to the brim.

Then pausing to rest on a rock before leaving,

She heard once again the Troll's sobbing and grieving.

Before she could move from her perch on the rock,

The rock began moving . . . and that was a shock!

Then into the clearing with one final bump,

Followed by one last tremendous big thump,

Stepped the giant Troll toddler, now smiling with glee.

He was back again with his giant Troll mother, you see!

Hulda was just about scared half to death,
But taking an extra big, special deep breath,
She screamed her most ear-splitting, spine-chilling scream —
The kind that could ripple a far-distant stream.

Holding their ears tight in pain and dismay,
The Trolls felt that Hulda should have her own way.
Stumbling and crashing, the two Trolls departed,
And Hulda was once again back where she started.

Her bucket was empty, though filled twice before.
She hurriedly started to fill it once more.
"The next time this happens," she solemnly vowed,
"I'll break my own record for screaming out loud!"

Just one final berry would now fill the bucket.

She reached out — but then — just before she could pluck it,

The world began bouncing about once again

And her blueberries sprinkled all over — but then

The sky became dark and the earth shook with thunder

And Hulda saw something that frightened and stunned her!

The mountain Troll father. Majestic! Titanic!
The one who, like Hulda, could always cause panic
Loomed over the treetops and finally found
The mean little girl with the horrible sound.
He shook a huge finger at Hulda, you see,
And pointed exactly to where she should flee.
Well, Hulda was terrified. Yes, that was true.
But Hulda knew very well just what to do.

She screamed and she screamed till she turned brilliant blue —
The world's greatest tantrum, the best she could do.
And it would have continued, except for one thing,
It just didn't bother the mountain Troll king.
Oh, he had a few shivers and it curled up his hair,
And his red and green eyes did widen and stare.
His jaw fell a little, but still, on the whole,
This was a very remarkable exceptional Troll!

Hulda's scream ended. It stopped at its peak,
When Hulda felt suddenly helpless and weak.
The Troll leaned in closer, a cautious amount,
He held up three fingers, and started to count.
So Hulda conceded . . . the Troll king had won.
Her tantrums were finished. Her screaming was done.

He continued his counting, now grinning with glee.
Hulda was gone when he got up to three.
He stood there a moment, not making a sound,
And then when he was sure there was no one around,
He quickly removed from his cavernous ears,
Two rocks he would treasure for many long years.
He guarded his secret with greatest concern,
Lest Hulda's big scream should chance to return.
But just to make sure, he prepared a surprise —
A gift for Miss Hulda of rather large size.

Yes, Hulda's big gift was the blueberry patch,
A gift no one ever could easily match.
He carefully moved it and left it that night
Where Hulda would see it by dawn's early light.

Well, of course, you can guess what the Troll had in mind,
Though in essence his gift was unselfish and kind.
He hoped now that Hulda would nevermore roam,
Now that her blueberry patch was near home.

And what of Miss Hulda — and how did she fare?

Well, she grew, and became something really quite rare.

A pleasant and soft-spoken lady was she

And lived very happily — fine as could be.

The gift from the king of the Trolls was the cue.

The kindness of others puts kindness in you.

Repaying in kind what to him was a pleasure

By goodness to others — the world's greatest treasure.